A Porcupine in a Pine Tree

A Canadian 12 Days of Christmas

Helaine Becker

illustrated by
Werner Zimmermann

Scholastic Canada Ltd.

Toronto New York London Auckland Sydney
Mexico City New Delhi Hong Kong Buenos Aires

Scholastic Canada Ltd.
604 King Street West, Toronto, Ontario M5V 1E1, Canada

Scholastic Inc.
557 Broadway, New York, NY 10012, USA

Scholastic Australia Pty Limited
PO Box 579, Gosford, NSW 2250, Australia

Scholastic New Zealand Limited
Private Bag 94407, Botany, Manukau 2163, New Zealand

Scholastic Children's Books
Euston House, 24 Eversholt Street, London NW1 1DB, UK

www.scholastic.ca

The paintings for this book were created in pencil,
ink and watercolour on Arches 90lb hot press paper.

Library and Archives Canada Cataloguing in Publication

Becker, Helaine, 1961-
A porcupine in a pine tree : a Canadian 12 days of Christmas / by
Helaine Becker ; illustrations by Werner Zimmermann.

ISBN 978-1-4431-2864-3 (pbk.)

1. Christmas--Juvenile poetry. 2. Canada--Juvenile poetry.
I. Zimmermann, H. Werner (Heinz Werner), 1951- II. Title.

PS8553.E295532P67 2013   jC811'.6   C2013-902045-4

6 5 4 3 2   Printed in Singapore 46   13 14 15 16 17

*To the greatest kids
in the world – Canadian kids!*
❧ H.B.

From a loving Grumpa to his darling Blipette.
❧ W.Z.

On the first day of Christmas,
My true love gave to me:
A porcupine in a pine tree.

On the second day of Christmas,
My true love gave to me:
Two caribou,
And a porcupine in a pine tree.

On the third day of Christmas,
My true love gave to me:
Three beaver tails,
Two caribou,
And a porcupine in a pine tree.

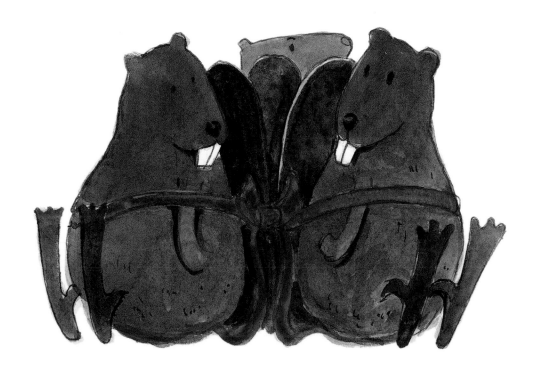

On the fourth day of Christmas,
My true love gave to me:
Four calling moose,
Three beaver tails,
Two caribou,
And a porcupine in a pine tree.

On the fifth day of Christmas,
My true love gave to me:
Five Stanley Cups,
Four calling moose,
Three beaver tails,
Two caribou,
And a porcupine in a pine tree.

On the sixth day of Christmas,
My true love gave to me:
Six squirrels curling,
Five Stanley Cups,
Four calling moose,
Three beaver tails,
Two caribou,
And a porcupine in a pine tree.

On the seventh day of Christmas,
My true love gave to me:

Seven sled dogs sledding,
Six squirrels curling,
Five Stanley Cups,
Four calling moose,
Three beaver tails,
Two caribou,
And a porcupine in a pine tree.

On the eighth day of Christmas,
My true love gave to me:
Eight Mounties munching,
Seven sled dogs sledding,
Six squirrels curling,
Five Stanley Cups,
Four calling moose,
Three beaver tails,
Two caribou,
And a porcupine in a pine tree.

On the ninth day of Christmas,
My true love gave to me:

Nine loons canoeing,
Eight Mounties munching,
Seven sled dogs sledding,
Six squirrels curling,
Five Stanley Cups,
Four calling moose,
Three beaver tails,
Two caribou,
And a porcupine in a pine tree.

On the tenth day of Christmas,
My true love gave to me:
Ten Leafs a-leaping,
Nine loons canoeing,
Eight Mounties munching,
Seven sled dogs sledding,
Six squirrels curling,
Five Stanley Cups,
Four calling moose,
Three beaver tails,
Two caribou,
And a porcupine in a pine tree.

On the eleventh day of Christmas,
My true love gave to me:
Eleven puffins piping,
Ten Leafs a-leaping,
Nine loons canoeing,
Eight Mounties munching,
Seven sled dogs sledding,
Six squirrels curling,
Five Stanley Cups,
Four calling moose,
Three beaver tails,
Two caribou,
And a porcupine in a pine tree.

On the twelfth day of Christmas,
My true love gave to me:
Twelve cubs a-dancing,
Eleven puffins piping,
Ten Leafs a-leaping,
Ninc loons canoeing,
Eight Mounties munching,
Seven sled dogs sledding,
Six squirrels curling,
Five Stanley Cups,
Four calling moose,
Three beaver tails,
Two caribou . . .

And a porcupine . . .

. . . in a . . .

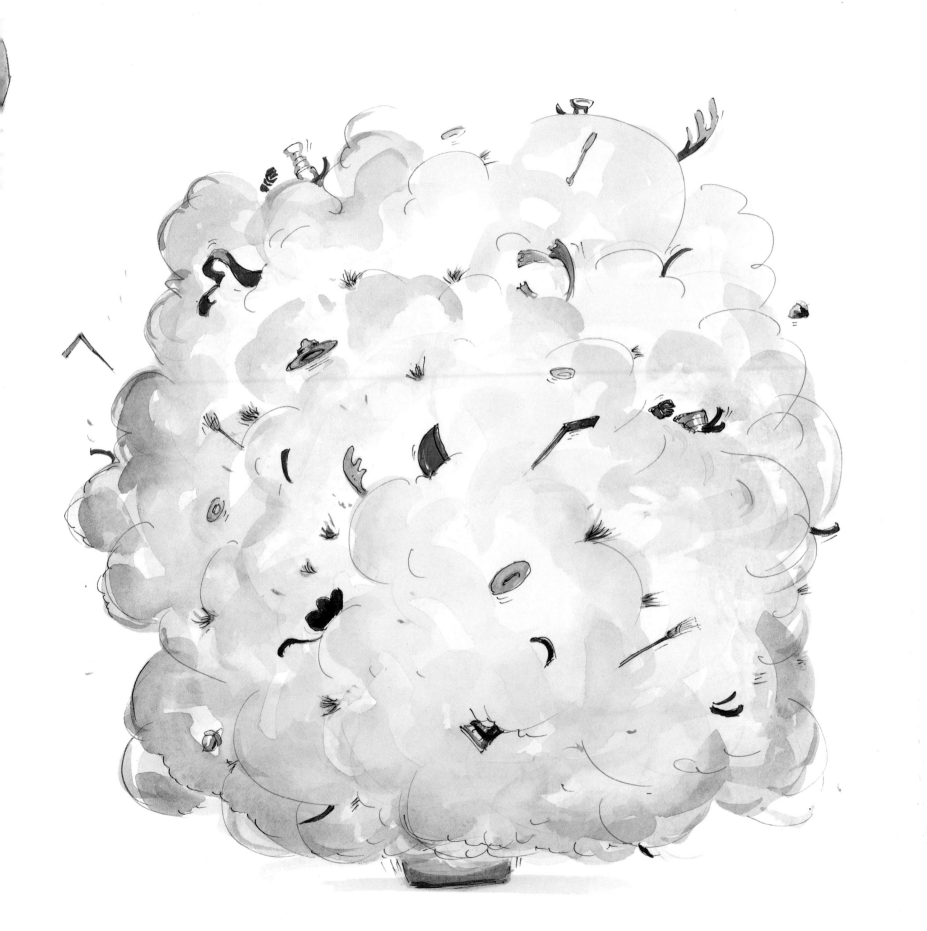

PINE TREE!